Wh(
To Be You?

by

Christine Sarno-Doyle

"Christine Sarno-Doyle has produced a book that whether
read with or by children, serves as a positive
affirmation and gives a potent message of acceptance."

—Maureen DiPalma
Reading and Special Education Teacher, Retired

SDP Publishing

Who's Going To Be You?, Published June, 2013

Interior and Cover Illustrations: Randy Jennings
Interior Layout: Howard Communigrafix, Inc.
Editorial and Proofreading: Eden Rivers Editorial Services
Photo Credits: Gayle Maziarz Casper

Published by SDP Publishing an imprint of SDP Publishing
Solutions, LLC.

For more information about this book contact Lisa Akoury-Ross
by email at lross@SDPPublishing.com.

To obtain permission(s) to use material from this work, please
submit a written request to:

SDP Publishing
Permissions Department
36 Captain's Way, East Bridgewater, MA 02333
or email your request to info@SDPPublishing.com.

Library of Congress Control Number: 2013930568

ISBN-13: 978-0-9885157-4-1

Printed in the United States of America

Acknowledgments

I wish to express my sincerest gratitude to the many loving souls who guided me along my journey. People who, to a little girl, a young woman, now a grandmother, had an extraordinary impact on her ability to survive, thrive, and be happy.

I've had my share of supporters and critics, and hold gratitude for each. For the critics, it was through the need to persevere that I learned how important it was to be true to my own unique self, which serendipitously allows me to love unconditionally. I am here after all to fulfill my destiny. Fitting in to a subjective norm is counter-intuitive for those, who even at a young age, feel an appreciation for uniqueness, but lack the vocabulary to communicate that which is in their hearts. A child's very being screams out, "This is not me!" when their inner voice is drowned out by a percussion of predetermined agendas. They learn to live a feigned existence. Fortunately today that norm has shifted, and we are more and more encouraging of our children's individuality—each as unique as their fingerprints and DNA.

To my supporters, those still with me and those who have passed on, you each forever hold a place in my heart. You were beacons along the way that shone light on a path and on the shadows. You encouraged me to find my own unique, eccentric self. I wish now to pay it forward. Follow your dreams and listen to your heart, for in their wisdom lies a destiny unique only to you.

I wish to thank Lisa Akoury-Ross, Literary Agent and Independent Publisher at SDP Publishing Solutions, LLC, and Lisa Ann Schleipfer at Eden Rivers Editorial Services. The past year has been incredible. Second time's a charm! From our initial conversation I felt that the connection was right, and your support and direction has confirmed that I was at the right place at the right time and in the best of hands. Howard Johnson, for your attention to and investment in all the details of layout and design. Randy Jennings, illustrator, and creative magician; again you brought my words to life.

For Giuseppe, Orion, Brooke, Kyle, Gabriella, Michaelena,
Olivia, Jake, Emma, Leah, Mary, Jared, Aaron, Gianna,
Samantha, Elizabeth, and Lyndsey.

When we are young, we learn so much as we grow, and we continue to learn and grow as we age. One of the most important lessons we can take hold of is to not judge ourselves by comparing ourselves to others. It's a relatively simple concept on its surface, but it's not always easy to follow. Everyone has strengths and weaknesses. If you see a quality that you admire in someone else, work on that part of yourself to develop it. But, don't think less of yourself because you don't possess that particular quality. You are your own person. You, my friend, have so many good qualities, I don't know how you keep them all inside. I admire you. Learn what strengths you hold, and use them to better yourself and others. Know your weak points and work to make them better. Be happy for yourself and for others. We are individuals, by definition that makes each of us original. So be one.

Trust your inner voice. It's also called your inner wisdom. Most of the answers you'll ever need about your life are right inside of you. It just takes practice to become aware of them. Practice listening to that wisdom. At night just before you go to sleep, ask a question for which you want an answer, about life, about you. Listen. The answer may come just as you are about to fall asleep. It may come as you wake in the morning, or it may come in some unexpected way during the day. You'll recognize the answer when it comes. (This doesn't work for test questions. You will have to study, and do your homework for those!)

Enjoy all that's new coming your way!
Believe in yourself!
Do your best!
Learn!
Laugh!
Love!

1
▼▼▼

"Ring around the rosy. A pocket full of posies!" The voices are jubilant, punctuated by the children's collective laughter. The carousel carries six of them, and more are scattered across the park. Jake and Olivia are helping Emma, who is climbing on the jungle gym. Brooke and Kyle are running through the spin-and-spray. Brie and Lena are swinging on the ropes. Their voices can be heard all the way across the field to the edge of the woods. A young girl sits watching under a tree, alone.

"They have so much energy," Darcie thinks. If they aren't spinning, 'round and 'round on the carousel, they're swimming, or climbing across the monkey bars, or up the jungle gym, or reaching their feet to the sky on the swing set. Leah and Mary have so much oomph, they look like they could blast off into space without any help at all!

"I don't like the carousel," Darcie says aloud as she watches the kids spinning and becoming one big blur as the wheel speeds up.

"I do like the swings," she says to herself as she watches the kids going higher with every pull on the chains. Darcie looks over at the monkey bars. "I think I like those best!" A big smile comes across her face. Darcie got to the other end of that horizontal ladder quicker than anyone else today. She found just the right rhythm to move quickly across those rungs, skipping some as she went. She beat Corey and Lila and even mean old Zack Benton, a feat she's very proud of.

Giuseppe jumps off the ropes and runs over to the jungle gym. Kyle is right behind him. "How can they keep going?" she wonders. No one else needs a break. Why does she?

"C'mon!" she hears the kids shout out from the carousel. They're calling her to join them. She shakes her head no as she calls back, "It makes me queasy!"

"C'mon!" she hears again as they spin towards her. "You big baby!" Zack shouts out as they spin away. Zack teases her a lot and that makes her sad, but she doesn't respond.

Standing near the carousel is a boy in Darcie's class at school. It's Orion. He's been watching the kids too, and by the way he's eyeing Zack she can tell Orion is bothered by Zack's teasing.

Orion lifts his hand and waves at Darcie and gives her a smile. Darcie waves back and sees him turn and walk towards the carousel. It has stopped now, and Orion's talking to Zack.

She can't hear what they're saying, but Orion and Zack both nod, and she sees Orion turn and start walking over to her.

"Hi," he says. "What are you doing?"

"Resting."

"Are you okay?"

"Yes, I'm all right."

"Don't mind Zack. He's just acting up. I asked him to stop teasing you."

Darcie nods her head as if to say, "Thank you." It is nice that Orion spoke up for her.

"All right, if you're okay, I'm going!" he says as he dashes off toward the pond. Jarod and Aaron are swimming, and he's going to jump in the water too. "See you later."

"See you later," Darcie replies. "Thank you!"

It's not right to tease or bully anyone. Darcie knows that, and most kids at the park know that too. They're learning. If they see someone

being teased or bullied, it's important to speak up and tell the person acting like a bully to stop. When they're uncomfortable speaking up, they can find an adult to talk to and explain what's happening.

"Darcie," her mom tells her, "speak up when you see someone being bullied. And, don't be afraid to speak up when someone is bullying you." Darcie knows the lesson, but she chose to be quiet today. She's feeling better resting in the shade, getting some relief from the midday heat.

"Maybe if I was more like the others no one would tease me," she thinks. Then she speaks her words aloud, imagining a genie somewhere might hear them and grant her what she wants! So, she sends her wish out on the wind. "I wish I could be more like them."

"Then who's going to be you?" a voice replies, and startles Darcie. She hasn't noticed anyone close enough to hear her speak! "It's Mr. Daily's voice," she thinks, and turns to see that yes, it is. It's Mr. Daily, the groundskeeper at Winnings Park, pruning the branches of nearby trees. There he is with his rolled-up cuffs hanging across the top of his work boots laced with those funny, bright-colored laces. "Funny for an old person to be wearing those," she thinks. "They look like little kid laces!" The pockets of his carpenter jeans are stuffed to their brims with supplies. The loose end of a roll of string dangles out of the top of one pocket, pressing against a grass-stained, yellow rag. The other side pocket reveals his sunglasses and a small pair of gardening shears, and what looks like a bottle of sun lotion that has never been opened.

"Hi, Mr. Daily," Darcie says with a smile.

"Hello, little lady," he replies.

Mr. Daily doesn't remember all the names of the boys and girls at the park so he refers to the girls as "ladies" and the boys as "gentlemen."

Everyone knows Mr. Daily, though. He's been at Winnings Park forever. Darcie's heard her mom and dad talk about him many times saying what a kind person he is, and that they appreciate how he watches out for the children while at the park.

"You taking a break?" he asks.

"Yes, it's too hot today."

"Take a break when you need to. You don't want to get overheated."

Overheated. Darcie hasn't heard that term before and thinks, "That's how I feel, overheated."

"It's not just that," Darcie says and pauses. "I can't keep up. They have so much more energy than I do."

Mr. Daily stops working when he hears Darcie continue to speak and steps out to listen. As he moves from behind the branches, Darcie fully sees his face. His skin is weathered from being in the sun so much. There's sweat across his forehead, and dirt on his nose and

15

around his cheeks. He's been hard at work today. His smile is bright though, and his eyes light up with his smile.

Mr. Daily's right arm hangs a bit limp. His left arm is stronger. Darcie never noticed any of his features before. All of these years she's been coming to the park and she never really looked at Mr. Daily. He's just always been there, like the playground toys. She really sees him today for the first time.

Mr. Daily kneels down on the edge of the shade where Darcie's sitting, and waits for her to continue speaking.

"Sometimes I would like to do other things," she tells him finally.

"You would?"

"Yes, but I don't, because no one else wants to do them with me. I don't like to be alone."

Looking out at the other kids, Mr. Daily shares an important lesson. "You know a lot of people don't like to be alone. But, I'll bet you wouldn't be alone for long. You'll meet someone who shares the same interests you do." He looks back at Darcie and offers her some encouragement. "Do yourself a favor; don't give up what you love to do. Spend some time here with everyone else if it makes you feel better. But, then take some time each day and do what you really enjoy doing."

"Do what I *really* enjoy doing." Darcie likes the sound of that. "Do what I really enjoy doing," she repeats and starts to think about the things she loves. She loves to be in her garden tending to her flowers. She loves to explore. She loves animals and nature. And her thoughts soon whisk her away into a daydream where she's surrounded by all she loves. She finds herself in an enchanted forest. It's peculiar here.

The sun is shining, yet rain is falling! Plants and flowers are getting needed sunshine and water at the same time! Wildflowers open, and roses bloom as she wanders near. "They're happy to see me," she fancies. Trumpet vines swirl around her shoulders, giving her a gentle hug, then twirl back in their place. She reaches for strawberries, and pixie dust suddenly glistens from her fingertips, and the berries burst to twice their size! *Oooo, they taste so sweet.* Lovebirds swoop by, and then return to light on her shoulder, whispering secrets of the forest in her ear. It's a magical, fairy-like place.

Darcie has a wonderfully creative imagination, and she continues along in her daydream until she hears Mr. Daily start to speak, and sees him pointing to the parking lot nearby.

"Do you see the Obaras over there?" he asks. Cris and Kevin Obara have arrived with their nieces and nephews for a day at the park. They're unpacking their van, carrying coolers of food and drinks that they share with all the kids. They have games to play, chairs to sit on, and a huge umbrella to use for shade.

"Yes, I see them," Darcie replies.

"When Kevin was young he spent a lot of time on his own."

"He did?"

"Yes. He was always going off doing other things."

"Like what?"

"I don't know exactly, but I know he loved animals. He'd go off on his own and the rest of us just kept playing. We knew he'd be back later."

"Did you make fun of him?"

"No. But, there were a couple of kids who did."

"Why?" asks Darcie.

Mr. Daily put down his rake and sat on the ground with Darcie. "Here's the lesson," he explains in a reassuring tone. "Each one of us is unique." He gestures to Darcie to look at all the people in the park. "Being unique means that we have our own interests. Sometimes what interests us will be the same as others, but sometimes our interests will be different. They can even be extraordinary. As we grow, we discover what those interests are. We discover what we love to do. We discover our passion and our talents. Some people learn earlier than others." He smiles and says, "Sounds like you're an early bloomer."

Darcie smiles too. "Bloomer. I like that," she thinks. "I'm blooming, like a flower."

"I want you to know that it didn't matter what anyone said to Kevin when he was young," Mr. Daily continues. "And, it doesn't matter what anyone may say to you or to me. There is nothing wrong with you doing what you love to do even if no one else wants to join you."

The wisdom this old man is sharing lightens Darcie's heart. "There isn't anything wrong with me doing what I love to do," she echoes with a hint of relief in her voice, "even if no one else wants to join me."

"The people who make fun of you are being mean and selfish," Mr. Daily explains.

"Selfish? I knew they were being mean, but I didn't know they were selfish!"

"Yes," he says, and Darcie sees him sit up straighter and pull his shoulders back a bit. "Let's say you would like to go for a walk and everyone else wants to play tag. Most kids are fine with your decision. They'll see you when you return. The kids who tease you are the ones who want everyone's attention on themselves, on what they are doing. That's selfish. They say mean things to get you to change your mind so that you will stay focused on them and what they want to do. Do you see? That's being mean *and* selfish."

"Kevin simply wanted to go and do things that interested him," Mr. Daily continues. "He loved being around animals." Darcie sees a big smile come on his face. "I think the animals knew he liked them too, because they would let him get *so* close. He'd sit very still and they'd get so close to him, we thought they'd hop right in his lap."

The picture of animals hopping into Kevin's lap makes Darcie and Mr. Daily start laughing.

"Yep, he's the best vet around. He's been happy all these years doing what he loves. No one's better at taking care of animals. Remember how he saved Leo?"

Darcie nods. She certainly remembers the
day on the bus when she saw Leo, the Caspers'
Saint Bernard, barrel out of the open gate in
their front yard. He ran right into the street.
She didn't see the car, but all the kids on the

bus heard tires screech and a loud thump. She knew Leo had been hit.

"If it wasn't for Kevin, who is now Dr. Obara, Leo may not have come home," Mr. Daily says, continuing his story. "When a person does what they love to do, there's no telling what good fortune will come their way, and what good fortune they will bring to others. It's the passion a person brings to the task that makes all the difference. That's what life's about. So, little lady, when you start wishing that you were someone else, you remember you have something special inside that no one else has. Ask yourself who's going to fulfill your dreams? Who's going to be you?"

Mr. Daily gives Darcie a big smile as he starts to rise and gets back to work, and she returns the smile with a nod that she understands him. "Take care, little lady," he calls out as he returns to his chores.

"Bye, Mr. Daily."

Darcie has forgotten all about not fitting in, and turns her attention back to the kids in the park. The others are playing a couple of made-up games. One is a type of baseball played with branches and leaves. The other is a game of golf where they use a branch for a golf club, and look for a round pinecone they can use for a ball.

Darcie's laughing as she watches them, and is thinking about what she wants to do next. "Do what I really enjoy doing," she reminds herself, and her thoughts take her into the woods, imagining what she may find there this time of year. What plants will be in bloom? What baby birds will be leaving their nests? Will she see one?

Just then a tiny sparrow swoops by so close to Darcie that she can feel its wings. Then again. She watches as the tiny sparrow lands near her feet. He's curiously inspecting a sliver of yellow fabric in the grass. "That must have come from Mr. Daily's rag," Darcie thinks as the bird looks up at her. "May I have this?" Darcie imagines the bird asking. "I could use this for my nest; it will help keep my babies warm." She sees the bird poke at it with its beak, then it hops on top of the cloth and looks up at Darcie, fluffing his feathers as if really waiting for permission.

"Of course you may have it," Darcie says aloud. And with that, she sees the sparrow lift the scrap and carry it away. He's headed toward the woods. Darcie decides to follow. "What exciting adventure will be in store for me today?" she wonders. Maybe the woodland sunflowers or wild violets will be in bloom!

The others are too busy to notice that she's leaving her spot in the shade, and is making her way to the path in the woods.

As she does, she thinks about what Mr. Daily said. *Do what you love.* "I will," she says, and she thinks about the questions he asked. *Who's going to fulfill your dreams? Who's going to be you?*

"Who's going to be me? But I am me!" she thinks. Darcie's thoughts soon turn to her surroundings. She loves the forest, and as she enters she puts aside the events of the day.

2

At dinner that evening Darcie tells her mom and dad about her day.

"Yes," her mom says. "Dr. Obara is a wonderful vet. He takes such good care of Emily and Sam." Emily and Sam are Darcie's two cats.

"I remember when we all played baseball together," her dad adds. "Kevin was exceptional. We all thought he'd go on to professional ball."

"He was better than you?" Darcie asks.

"That he was!"

"But, you're a coach!" Darcie states with more of a question in her voice. She's looking curiously at her father as he explains, "I loved to play baseball. I still do. But, some people just have a natural talent, and Kevin was a natural," he pauses, and then with a smile and a wink at Darcie he admits, "I wasn't."

Darcie's smiling back, nodding that she understands.

"We had a great team and we had a lot of fun. I still love the game. That's why I've been coaching all these years. I found a way to continue doing something I love. I'm happy, and maybe in the process I can help others discover what makes them happy doing what they love to do."

"Life lesson honey," her mom says. "Discover what it is you're passionate about. Everyone is passionate about something. When you have your answer, do as much with it as you can."

"Quite a lot for one day," her dad says. "You'll be fine."

Darcie leaves the dinner table and goes outside to spend time in her garden. Her red watering can in hand, and filled to the brim, she heads to her hideaway in the backyard. It's her fairy garden, full of colorful plants and flowers she selected and planted herself. Two birdhouses sit at its entrance, and small, fairy figurines line its winding walkway. A favorite bench sits in a corner of the garden where Darcie sits and reads. And a marble birdbath in the garden's center provides a cool and refreshing spot for birds and animals.

Darcie loves her special place and Darcie loves to imagine. So, as she's watering her flowers she muses, "What if fairy dust came out of the spout, and sprinkled on the flowers instead of water? Flower buds would open and close in delight! The berries would glisten. The petunias would twirl. Pansies would dance. What fun that would be!"

Then, just as she notices the last drop of water fall from the spout, Darcie takes a

moment to look around at all she created, and she sees that it is just as beautiful without the magic!

It's the end of a wonderful day full of surprises, make-believe, and lessons.

3
▼▼▼

The next morning, Darcie is up and on her way to the park. She travels the same path every time. It starts at the end of her street, and winds through the woods along the edge of Winnings Pond. The path is well traveled, though for her it feels like a private pathway. Others may walk and run along the trail, but Darcie feels a part of it. She knows every hollow, every breach made by the large roots that stretch across the path, the moss that grows on the north side of the tree bark, ferns and mushroom patches on the ground, and all the large rocks along the way.

She knows the path so well that if she closes her eyes she can still see it in her mind. The trail is surrounded by acres of towering trees and interweaving branches. The large oak trees have narrow-shaped leaves and plenty of acorns. The maple trees have wider-shaped leaves with three large tips, and plenty of fruit. It's not the kind of fruit you eat. The maple tree fruit are long, bunny-ear-shaped flora the kids call helicopters—because when the fruit falls it spins 'round and 'round through the air. The fruit are actually maple tree seeds that will land in other parts of the forest and take root.

There are many more evergreens than deciduous trees, those that lose their leaves. And, there are a variety of bushes and brush that the animals feed on, eating leaves and berries.

Last spring she noticed that a large tree had fallen during the winter. When she saw it on the ground she went to look at where the break had occurred. As she studied its trunk, she counted its rings to determine how old it was. How long had this tree been in the forest? Some of the rings were not clear, but she did her best to count those she could identify. "Fifty, at least fifty," she said. The tree was at least fifty years old.

There are many sounds along the path, and a loud chirp gets her attention. "I know that one!" she says aloud as she looks up into the branches for a cardinal. There's not enough light, though. Clouds are blocking the sun. "I wish I could see you," Darcie says. Then, as if the genie hears her and is granting her wish, a gust of wind shifts the clouds, and sunlight comes through the tree tops.

"There you are," Darcie says with a big smile. She's spotted a female cardinal sitting on a branch high above. It's the female cardinal for sure because her colors are muted. Her feathers are not as red as her male companion's. "Where's your friend?" Darcie asks. She can hear another cardinal nearby, and as she watches, a bright-red cardinal swoops over and lands on the branch next to the female. "There he is," she says. The birds stay together on the branch for a moment, and then together take flight.

She doesn't see them any longer, but she can still hear them. She's happy just to listen. As she listens to an assortment of chirping going on around her, she tries to identify those she can. She is able to distinguish the noisy call of the blue jays, and the lamenting sound of the mourning doves. She can hear the cheery song of the warbler, and the flute-like sound of the wood thrush. That's five she has recognized today! "Where's the sparrow that flew off with the piece of yellow fabric yesterday?" she wonders. Darcie loves this pastime, so she decides to stay for a while and makes herself comfortable on a mound of leaves that have collected just off of the trail.

As she enjoys the birds she remembers the story Mr. Daily told her about Kevin Obara. *If I sit very still, I wonder if any animals will come up close to me.* So, she waits.

No animals yet, but she does notice little creatures scurrying around on the ground over and under leaves and twigs. "I don't recognize those bugs," she thinks, and then quickly corrects herself: "Insects, they are insects." A fact she learned in school.

"Eeyuu, what are those?" She squirms. Two large, strange-looking beetles rush past her

heading somewhere. She doesn't know where. She's just glad they are in a hurry to move along.

"How on earth can tiny ants carry such big pieces?" she wonders as she watches a line of ants going about their daily chores. "What are they doing with all that stuff they're carrying?"

A chipmunk darts past. Then another—this one stops and looks back at Darcie. He's looking for food. He's not afraid of her at all. A few seconds tick by, and then he runs off just as fast as he arrived. She smiles as she watches him dart through the brush, over a large log, and then disappear.

Just as she loses sight of the chipmunk something else catches her eye. There is light reflecting off a tiny pair of eyes peering out from under the log the chipmunk just maneuvered his way across.

"What is it?" she wonders.

They aren't moving. She's not sure she wants them to move.

Darcie remains very still and watches.

A minute passes. Two, three minutes have passed.

Neither Darcie nor the pair of eyes has moved. Those eyes haven't even blinked! Darcie tries not to blink either. She doesn't want to miss anything if those eyes should move even the slightest bit. It's been too long now, and Darcie can't hold her stare any longer. She blinks! And in that instant, a burst of wind sweeps by and a muffled voice can be heard uttering, "Whaat aare yoouu dooooing?" She doesn't know what it is, but something has just propelled itself out of the tiny space under the log.

Darcie is startled and jumps back from her seat on the ground. She's ready to get up and run, but she sees that what has just exploded from out of the darkness has come to a stop.

She watches as the creature starts to shake itself, behaving like her dog when it shakes water off its fur. This animal isn't shaking water off its body, though. It is ridding itself of dirt, and it's making a mess! There is dust and dirt everywhere!

As the dust cloud begins to settle, Darcie is able to make out the creature's color, its size, and its shape. It is brown. It has white markings. It has sharp pin points among its fur. It's a porcupine!

"Sorry," says the porcupine as he looks over at Darcie. "Hope I didn't scare you."

Darcie doesn't answer. This is strange. *Is he really speaking?*

"My name's Perry," he says. "What's your name?"

Darcie still doesn't answer.

"It's easier for me to come out from the other side," Perry continues. "But, it's fun trying to see how far I can propel myself out of the hole on this side. I can really get some distance when I hold my breath and blow out real fast. One time I landed where you're sitting! Did I scare you? I hope I didn't scare you."

Darcie still is not speaking.

"Can you talk?" Perry asks. "I don't come out during the day. I come out at night. But, you woke me and you've been here for a while. I thought I'd come out and see if you are lost. Are you lost?"

"Yyyes," Darcie says slowly.

"You're lost?" Perry asks.

"No, I'm not lost," Darcie answers. "Yes, I can talk."

"This is not normal," Darcie thinks to herself, and wonders if animals spoke to Dr. Obara too!

"What are you doing here?" Perry asks a lot of questions.

"I like it here."

"You one of us? You don't look like one of us."

"What do you mean?"

"Are you an animal?" Perry chuckles. He knows she's not an animal.

"I'm not an animal!" Darcie replies, quickly correcting Perry. "I'm a person!"

"Hey, nothing wrong with being an animal!" Perry proclaims.

"Yeah, I know. I love animals. I'm just not one."

"Why are you staying so long today?"

"I like it here."

"Yeah? Me too. Why are you alone? Where are your other persons?"

"People."

"Huh?"

"It's people. You should have asked, 'Where are your other people?' People are many. Person is just one. I'm a person." Darcie

wonders, "Why am I explaining grammar to a porcupine?"

Perry's sitting, curiously looking at Darcie.

"The others are playing at the park," she continues.

"Oh," Perry says, and then turns and starts rummaging for something to eat.

"I'm taking my time. I like it here in the woods," she says. "Anyway, I'm not in a hurry to get to the park. I'm uncomfortable there sometimes. I don't always fit in with the others."

"Huh?" Perry's confused. "What does that mean? 'Don't fit in.'"

"I'm different."

"You're supposed to be different."

"Maybe, but I'm too different. Sometimes

I get teased because I'm not like everyone else and that makes me feel sad. I want to be more like them."

"I don't understand. How can you be like others and still be you?"

"I am me. I just want to be more like the other kids too."

"Impossible! You can't be two people at the same time. Can you?" Perry's looking at Darcie with surprise. "Is that magic?"

Darcie doesn't answer, so Perry turns and continues to look for food.

"What is he doing?" she wonders.

"Seems to me that it's impossible for

you to be something you're not," Perry says with his nose in the dirt. "Anyway, if you want to be someone else, who's going to be you?"

"All I know is that sometimes I'm uncomfortable being around the other kids. And, sometimes I don't like being me."

A new voice bellows out from behind the bush next to Darcie. "Well that's the most ridiculous thing I ever heard!" All the commotion had gotten Stuart's attention.

Darcie looks over to see who is talking and shrieks, "Oh my goodness...! A skunk!"

Stuart sits calmly and keeps looking at Darcie. "You say that like it's a bad thing, I'm not a bad thing!" he replies.

"Don't spray! Are you going to spray me?"

"Calm down, Missy."

"My name's Darcie."

"Calm down, Miss Darcie. I don't go around spraying every new thing I see; lucky for you. I have to save my odorous defending lotion for dangerous creatures! Are you dangerous?" Stuart asks as he turns and starts to raise his tail.

"She's not dangerous," says Perry, then turns and looks at Darcie. "You're not dangerous are you?"

Darcie is shaking her head. "No."

"Then, Miss Darcie, you really need

to lighten up. What's this about not belonging? Everyone belongs, even *him*." Stuart is pointing to Perry, who mumbles with a mouth full of food, "Yeah even me." Perry is more interested in finding more to snack on now that Stuart has picked up the conversation.

Darcie looks over at Perry. "That wasn't nice! Did he hurt your feelings?"

"Who?"

"Stuart."

"When?"

"Just now when he said, 'Everyone belongs, *even him*,' like you're different, or not good enough. Didn't that make you feel bad?"

"No," answers Perry. "I *am* different. I'm supposed to be different. We're all different. Who else do you know who has this type of fur?" Perry is pulling on one of his quills and letting it snap back into place.

"That's not fur!" Stuart quickly replies.

Stuart looks at Darcie, and points out that Perry has quills. "Have you ever touched one of those things? He's a walking pin cushion! This is fur!" Stuart says as he runs his paw over his soft, black coat with its distinctive white stripe. "Soft and luxurious—this is what you call fur," he says, proudly primping himself.

Perry grins. "He doesn't like it when I call mine fur."

Stuart sighs and shakes his head. "And,

look at these colors. Isn't this combination beautiful?" He's still admiring himself.

"I'm glad we're different. Who wants to be the same as a skunk? No thank you," Perry pipes up.

"Keep it up, Perry!" Stuart warns as he pretends to turn and raises his tail.

"Just kidding, Stuart."

"Yeah, I know," Stuart says. "You see, Miss Darcie. I don't want to be him and he doesn't want to be me. Why do you want to be someone else? If you're anybody else, who's going to be you?"

Darcie's thinking. *Who's going to be you?* That's the same question Mr. Daily and Perry asked. It's the same thing Mom and Dad were talking about last night.

"Do you hear that?" Stuart asks, making reference to all the sounds in the forest. "The birds are singing and chirping. They each have a special sound. Wouldn't it be dull if they all sang the same song or if they all looked the same? You have a special song and a special look too! It just wouldn't be the same if they sounded the same." Stuart stops and thinks about what he just said.

"Hey that's a good title for a song! *It Just Wouldn't Be The Same If They Sounded The Same.* Get it? Hey Perry!" Stuart is laughing because he made a joke, and starts singing the words to a familiar beat. "It just wouldn't be the same, if they sounded the same. Dear Darcie. Dear Darcie. Ha ha ha ha. Yeah, this is great!"

Perry waddles over and joins in the singing, "Dear Darcie, Dear Darcie. That's good Stuart! Ha ha ha. You see, Dear Darcie. It's great being different. Hey, look at this!" And he takes one of his quills and starts to floss his teeth. "No one else can do this," he says, and displays a big grin.

Stuart raises his paws in the air and rolls his eyes. "He's right, though. I couldn't have quills. How would I raise my tail

to spray my very own brand of odorous defending lotion if I had quills? I'd stab myself in the butt!"

Perry hears that and looks up at Stuart, and then over at Darcie, and they all start laughing.

"Differences make us interesting. Don't you want to be interesting, Miss Darcie?" Stuart asks.

"Yes, I just don't want to be *so* different."

"No can do, Missy. You are."

4
▼▼▼

"The things that make us different allow us to view life from our own unique perch," another voice in the forest joins in.

"Hey Brandy," Stuart calls. A blue bird is sitting on the branch above.

"Hi, Brnnnday," mumbles Perry with his cheeks full of food.

"Differences *are* important," Brandy says. "For instance, I can spot danger from way up here and sound an alarm for everyone in the forest to be careful, or to run or hide. If Stuart sees or smells something menacing, he can use his looks to scare it away, especially if he raises his tail."

"Huh?" Perry's head pops up. He just heard Brandy say Stuart's looks are scary

and thinks that's funny. "Ha ha ha. Yeah, his looks *are* awful," Perry says, rolling on the ground laughing.

"That's not what I meant," Brandy corrects Perry and turns back to Darcie. "The animals learn pretty fast that if they see that stripe they could get sprayed with a very strong odor, and it will last for a long time."

"Yeah," Stuart says proudly.

"It smells pretty bad around here too afterwards, but Stuart helps himself and the rest of us when he feels he needs to use it," Perry says, catching his breath from laughing.

"And, Perry can scare a predator when he shows his quills. Something else, Perry's sloppy eating habits help others too. Do you see all that food he's dropping?" Brandy asks.

Perry's eyes open wide as he looks over at Darcie. His cheeks are stuffed with food and some of it is dropping on the ground around him.

"Even his sloppy eating has a way of helping others," Brandy explains. "Fellows like Perry spend a lot of time sitting in trees, and when they drop food on the ground other animals come along and find it. It's

really helpful in the winter when food is scarce. It's a way of sharing I guess."

Darcie is starting to understand that differences are important. She's looking around observing all the distinct qualities nearby, just like the game she plays when she looks at similar pictures and tries to find what's different or the same between them.

As Darcie explores her surroundings, Brandy continues her lesson on the diversity in nature. "Does the maple tree wish it were the plant life below? Probably not. The maple tree needs the sun and so its branches bear the heat, and provide shade for all that is underneath. That's how it's made. Do the pine trees wish they could shed their pine needles in the winter like the deciduous trees? Probably not. The snow on the pine limbs can sometimes be too heavy, and a branch will snap and fall. But the pine branches provide protection for the animals and other living things in the forest. It's necessary. That's how it's made."

Darcie spies moss on the ground. "What about moss?" she asks. "It's so small. What value does moss hold?"

"It has value too," Brandy replies. "Yes, it is short as plant life goes, and because it's small one might think it has less value than other plants, but that would be incorrect. Moss is critical to life in the forest. It keeps moisture in the soil and it holds nutrients that we need to live. Animals and plants depend on moss. Do you see? Everything has value. Everything is important."

This is all making sense to Darcie, and she's starting to realize that unique features are things to be grateful for and to be excited about.

That's what Mom and Dad were talking

about. That's what Mr. Daily was talking about. *Who's going to be me? I have to pay attention to what makes me special so that I can be my best too!*

"Just like Dr. Obara who takes care of all the animals. Just like Officer Henry who helps us on our way to school. Ms. Angela who teaches us in class, Ms. Caley who takes our photographs, Dr. Joe and Nurse Liz, Mr. Derick at the diner, and Ms. Jess at the bakery. Artists, scientists, everyone, everywhere! Different! Wonderful! Just like Perry, Stuart, and Brandy!"

Her smile grows bright and her eyes sparkle. She is so happy that in her glow, the forest lights up and glistens.

Darcie's heart grows light.

5

Children's voices can be heard in the distance making their way down the path. Daylight is waning, and Darcie wonders, "How long have I been here?" Gazing at her new friends, she says, "They must be getting close."

"You just heard that?" Stuart asks Darcie.

"Yes!" Darcie says with surprise. She hasn't heard them at all until now.

"Yeah, I've been listening for a while," Perry says. "They're getting closer. And one of them smells awful! What have they been doing? Playing with one of Stuart's relatives?" He starts laughing and Stuart gives him a smirk.

"Their sense of hearing and smell are better than humans'," Brandy adds. "We all

knew your friends were coming this way. We should go now."

Darcie turns toward the path to see if the children are in sight then spins back to Perry, Stuart, and Brandy. *What will the others think if they see me sitting here with a porcupine, a skunk, and a bird? What should we do?* But they're not sitting with her anymore. She looks up to see that only Brandy has returned to her perch on the branch above. The forest is humming as if nothing extraordinary happened today.

"Hey Darcie, what are you doing?" Olivia calls out as she runs up. "Missed you today. Where've you been?"

"We're going to Jake and Emma's house for a cookout. You know how great those are! You coming?" Guiseppe asks. "C'mon! Come with us!" he calls out as he continues to run down the trail.

"I'll be along in a while," Darcie answers and the kids continue on.

Following right behind the children is Mr. Daily. He's making sure everyone is safely finding their way home.

"Hi little lady," he says, greeting Darcie.

"I didn't see you in the park today. Have you been here all day?" Mr. Daily asks. He's stopped and is looking around like he's waiting for something. Or is he waiting for someone? "Let me guess. You had company."

Darcie's expression is surprise. "What should I say? Does he know?" she wonders, and then asks, "Do you know?"

Mr. Daily nods his head.

It's not too long before Perry appears, waddling out from the far side of his log.

He decided to walk out this time instead of propelling himself out with a wad of dirt.

"Hey," says Perry.

"Hey yourself," Mr. Daily replies.

"You know him?" Darcie asks.

"Yes, we all know Perry. Don't we buddy?"

Perry's moving along, nodding his head.

"We?"

"Yes, many people know Perry."

"How?" she asks.

"It seems that this is a special place for

a lot of people. Over the years many have stopped here to reflect on the very questions you've been asking lately. 'How do I fit in? Why am I different?' When we try to find answers to such important questions, we choose a place to stop for a while and reflect. Did you find some answers today?"

A slight grin has replaced the worry on Darcie's face and she nods, "Yes."

"Most of the answers we'll ever need about our life come from right inside our heart." He continues, "Others come from the most extraordinary places," and winks at Perry. "We need only be still for a while so we can listen."

"Listen to what?" she asks. "Perry?"

"Life can get very busy and we lose sight of what's important to us. We try too hard to be like everyone else or to be someone we're not. That's when we become disconnected from our own dreams. It's important to take time to be still and listen to your heart. Your heart will always lead you back to where you belong. It's another lesson we learn as we grow."

Perry motions to Darcie, "See, he knows."

"And then there are the messages we get from others or other extraordinary places. Perry knew why you were here." He turns to Perry. "'Who's going to be you?' Is that what you asked her?"

Perry nods yes.

"Stuart and the others?"

"Yes. It was a very pleasant afternoon," Perry says proudly.

"Well then, little lady. I have no doubt. You will be just fine. Don't forget all you learned today. And, if you ever feel lost, remember your special place." He smiles at Darcie, and waves good-bye to Perry and continues on his way home.

Perry says good-bye and returns to his spot under the log.

Darcie stays for a little while longer reflecting on the events of the day, and thinking about all she's learned.

"This was magical! Have I been daydreaming all afternoon?" she wonders. "Was this my imagination or was this real?"

She rises from the cushion of leaves that provided her a comfortable place to rest and thinks about all the joy she experienced. "I learned so much today. Differences are important. Everyone and everything has value. Everyone and everything has something significant to offer. It is real."

"I *am* different," she says. "And that's okay. I am me and no one else, and no one else can be me!" She turns to see her friends, now far down the path. "They are who they are supposed to be too."

"If I ever start to doubt myself again, I hope I remember this day. But, then how could I ever forget?"

Darcie glances over at Perry, whose eyes are peering out from the darkness under the log where she first met them.

"I am so glad you came out and spoke with me today," she tells him.

Perry blinked his little porcupine eyes in acknowledgment.

Then, Darcie turns and heads home.

Stepping out at the end of her own private pathway, Darcie whispers a message and sends it out on the wind, "Thank you. Thank you so much. That was extraordinary, make believe or not."

The cool breeze carries a whisper back, "Who's going to be you?"

Her happy heart answers what she knows for sure, "I am."

The End

About The Author

Christine Sarno-Doyle is an author and inspirational writer who has published a number of motivational articles. She describes her writing purpose as a means to empower others, specifically in their quest to discover and focus on their individuality. "I'm all about personal growth and empowerment, and my hope is that what I offer will inspire others. For children, learning to value themselves can never come too early." Widowed at nineteen after losing her mother at fifteen, Christine says that she struggled with her own sense of self early on and since that, "It's always been important to me to reach out and help others with their sense of belonging and self-esteem."

Before becoming a full-time writer, Christine's career included development, marketing communications, and public relations. At the age of 45 she graduated Cum Laude from the University of Massachusetts with a Bachelor's of Science in Criminal Justice followed by a first year of law studies at Massachusetts School of Law at Andover. Health issues cut short her legal career and brought about a reassessment of her goals. Christine decided it was time to return to her first love: writing, and to follow her dream of becoming a published author.

More information about Christine Sarno-Doyle, her writings, and her inspirational articles can be found at her website: www.ChristineSarnoDoyle.com.

 **SDP Publishing**

Other children's books by Christine Sarno-Doyle

Your Inside Shape, Children's book, ages 4-8.

Available at:

Amazon.com

BarnesAndNoble.com

SDPPublishingSolutions.com

For our complete bookstore list please visit us at:

www.SDPPublishingSolutions.com

Contact us at: info@SDPPublishing.com

CPSIA information can be obtained
at www.ICGtesting.com
Printed in the USA
BVIC00n1212190114
342305BV00001B/1